SON
I WROTE
THIS BOOK
ABOUT
YOU

THIS BOOK
WAS
WRITTEN BY

....

....

....

YOU ARE GOOD AT

....

....

....

YOU ARE SUPER AWESOME BECAUSE

....

....

....

I LOVE HOW YOU

. . . .

. . . .

. . . .

OUR FAVORITE THING TO DO TOGETHER IN SUMMER IS

....

....

....

YOU ALWAYS
HELP ME TO

....

....

....

I LOVE WHEN YOU COOK

....

....

....

YOU LAUGH A LOT
WHEN I

....

....

....

YOU ARE SMARTER THAN

....

....

....

YOU WORK HARD AT

....

....

....

I LOVE WHEN YOU

....

....

....

MY FAVORITE THING ABOUT YOU IS

....

....

....

BEST THING ABOUT YOUR JOB IS

....

....

....

OUR FAVORITE THING TO DO TOGETHER IS

....

....

....

I WOULD BUY YOU A MILLION

....

....

....

YOUR FAVORITE FOOD IS

....

....

....

YOU LOVE WHEN I

....

....

....

MOVIE/TV SHOW THAT WE BOTH LOVE IS

. . . .

. . . .

. . . .

OUR FAVORITE THING TO DO TOGETHER IN WINTER IS

. . . .

. . . .

. . . .

YOU ARE STRONGER THAN

....

....

....

YOU LOVE ME BECAUSE

. . . .

. . . .

. . . .

I HAVE NEVER SEEN YOU

. . . .

. . . .

. . . .

YOU ARE SPECIAL TO ME BECAUSE

....

....

....

YOU MAKE EVERYONE

....

....

....

YOU WILL ALWAYS BE MY

....

....

....

YOU TAUGHT ME HOW TO

....

....

....

I LOVE WHEN YOU TELL STORIES ABOUT

....

....

....

YOU INSPIRE ME TO DO

....

....

....

I LOVE WHEN WE PRANK

. . . .

. . . .

. . . .

I LOVE YOU A LOT
BECAUSE YOU NEVER

....

....

....

FUNNIEST THING YOU DO IS

. . . .

. . . .

. . . .

OUR FAVORITE THING TO DO TOGETHER IN SPRING IS

....

....

....

I WAS AMAZED WHEN
YOU FIXED MY

....

....

....

I FEEL SAFE WHEN YOU

....

....

....

YOU DON'T CARE ABOUT

. . . .

. . . .

. . . .

I'M PROUD TO SAY YOU ARE

....

....

....

YOU LIKE TO

....

....

....

OUR FAVORITE THING TO DO TOGETHER IN AUTUMN IS

....

....

....

I LOVED WHEN YOU SURPRISED ME WITH

....

....

....

YOU ALWAYS SAY

....

....

....

I LOVE YOU MORE THAN

....

....

....

GAME I LIKE TO PLAY
WITH YOU IS

....

....

....

YOU ARE PROUD OF ME WHEN I

....

....

....

YOU ARE A PERFECT

. . . .

. . . .

. . . .

I WANT YOU TO KNOW
THAT I WILL

....

....

....

I LOVE IT WHEN YOU

....

....

....